For Amelia, Louisa, Adam and Phoebe Deering —A.R.
For my kitties, Zipper & Velcro —V.v.d.B.

Whoo! Whoo! Goes the Train Text copyright © 2009 by Anne Rockwell Illustrations copyright © 2009 by Anne Rockwell and Vanessa van der Baan Manufactured in China. All rights reserved. No part of this book may be used or reproduced in any manner whatsoever without written permission except in the case of brief quotations embodied in critical articles and reviews. For information address HarperCollins Children's Books, a division of HarperCollins Publishers, 10 East 53rd Street, New York, NY 10022. www.harpercollinschildrens.com Library of Congress Cataloging-in-Publication Data Rockwell, Anne F. Whoo! Whoo! Goes the train / story and illustrations by Anne Rockwell ; with colorization by Vanessa van der Baan.—1st ed.   p. cm. Summary: Allan, who loves trains and learns all that he can about them, has a wonderful time when he finally takes his first train ride. ISBN 978-0-06-056227-4 (trade bdg.) — ISBN 978-0-06-056228-1 (lib. bdg.) [1. Railroads—Trains—Fiction. 2. Voyages and travels—Fiction.] I. Title.
PZ7.R5943Wh 2009 2003011101 [E]—dc22 CIP AC
Designed by Shira M. Cohen
09 10 11 12 13 SCP 10 9 8 7 6 5 4 3 2 ❖ First Edition

Whoo! Whoo! Goes the Train!

Story and illustrations by Anne Rockwell
with colorization by Vanessa van der Baan

HarperCollinsPublishers

Allan loved trains. His favorite toy was a little wooden train. He had train books and posters as well as a CD of train noises. But Allan had never ridden on a real train.

Allan made trains out of his cereal. He'd go "Whooooo-whooo!" so that he sounded just like a train—sometimes with his mouth full.

He took his time getting dressed or getting ready
for bed if he was pretending to be a semaphore.

Every week, Allan went to the library to borrow books about trains. On the way was a train crossing. Allan always hoped the gate would be down.

Clang! Clang!

The bell meant a train was coming. Sometimes a long freight train with boxcars and shiny tanker cars came rolling and rumbling along.

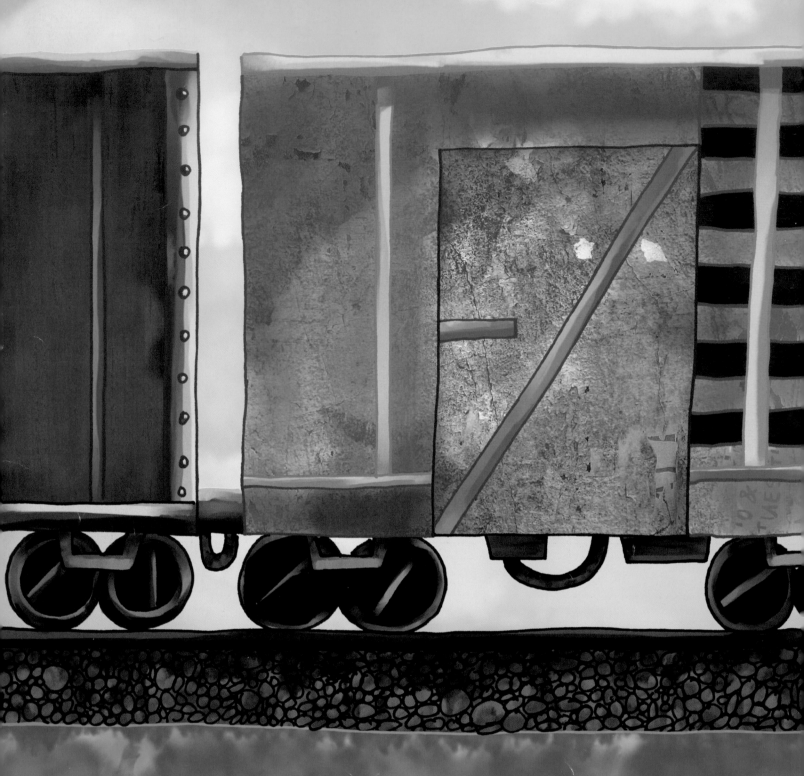

There were **red** boxcars,
green ones,
and **yellow** ones.

There were always more freight cars than Allan could count.

One day, Allan and his parents drove to a small building right next to the railroad tracks.

A high-speed passenger train went whishing past. They were at the train station!

"Allan, get ready for your first train ride," said Dad.

"Whooooo-whooo!"

Allan couldn't wait.

Dad bought tickets. Allan wiggled on the bench,
but he held tight to his ticket.

"When is the train coming?" he asked again and again.
"It's almost time," said his mom.

And then it was time. Everyone went outside.
A passenger train slowed down and came to a stop.

Whoosh!

The door slid open, and the conductor stepped out.
"All aboard!" he cried.

As soon as everyone got on the train, the door slid shut and the engine started up.

Allan saw a sign for a bathroom at the end of the car. He wanted to go. He'd never been to the bathroom on a train.

When he and his dad came back
from the bathroom, the conductor
punched a hole in Allan's ticket.
   "This is my first train ride," Allan
told him proudly.
   "Good for you!" said the conductor.

Clickety-clack.

The train went past a crossing.
   Allan waved to the people waiting for
the train to pass.

He watched buildings race by his window.

Below the tracks, cars drove underneath a railroad bridge.

KT-123

Suddenly, everything was **black**.

The train was going through a tunnel.

When the train rolled out of the tunnel,
Allan saw **blue** sky, **white** clouds,
and cows in a **green** field.
The train went *faster* and *faster*.

It crossed a long, long bridge over a river.
  A freight train going in the opposite direction
passed them.

As Allan ate his hot dog and popcorn, his dad closed his eyes and went to sleep. Allan's mother read her book.

But Allan was having fun watching things whiz by his window.

When the train slowed down and stopped, Allan's dad jumped up. Allan was sad that the train ride had ended. He could have gone on riding all day and all night.

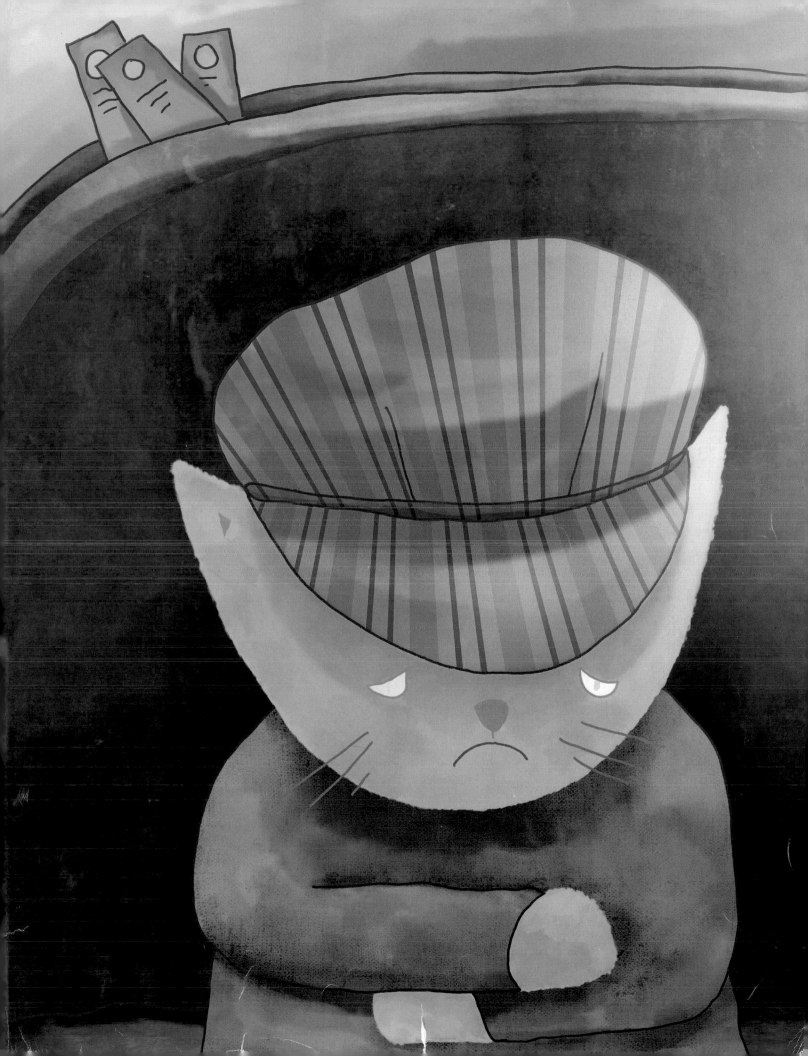

And then, everywhere he looked Allan saw trains going this way and that—going

Whoo! Whoo! and Clickety-clack.

WELCOME TO TRAINLAND

Allan rode the old-fashioned steam locomotive first.

That was his favorite. He was very, very happy.